Nature's Super Secrets

# Why Does the Sun Set?

By Violet Miller

 **Gareth Stevens**
Publishing

Please visit our website, www.garethstevens.com. For a free color catalog of all our high-quality books, call toll free 1-800-542-2595 or fax 1-877-542-2596.

**Library of Congress Cataloging-in-Publication Data**

Miller, Violet, 1982-
  Why does the sun set? / Violet Miller.
    p. cm. — (Nature's super secrets)
  Includes index.
  ISBN 978-1-4339-8181-4 (pbk.)
  ISBN 978-1-4339-8182-1 (6-pack)
  ISBN 978-1-4339-8180-7 (library binding)
  1. Sun—Rising and setting—Juvenile literature. I. Title. II. Series: Nature's super secrets.
  QB216.M55 2013
  523.7—dc23
                                                    2012030516

Published in 2013 by
**Gareth Stevens Publishing**
111 East 14th Street, Suite 349
New York, NY 10003

Copyright © 2013 Gareth Stevens Publishing

Designer: Nicholas Domiano
Editor: Sarah Machajewski

Photo credits: Cover, p.1 Hollygraphic/Shutterstock.com; p. 5 (right) 1000 Words/Shutterstock.com; pp. 5 (left), 15 Elenamiv/Shutterstock.com; p. 7 lexaarts/Shutterstock.com; p. 9 J. McPhail/Shutterstock.com; p. 11 Dorling Kindersley/Getty Images; p. 13 (statue) upthebanner/Shutterstock.com; p. 13 (Hong Kong) Khoroshunova Olga/Shutterstock.com; p. 17 Vibrant Image Studio/Shutterstock.com; p. 19 S.Borisov/Shutterstock.com; p. 21 ColorsArk/Shutterstock.com

Printed in the United States of America

CPSIA compliance information: Batch #CW13GS: For further information contact Gareth Stevens, New York, New York at 1-800-542-2595.

# Contents

**Boldface** words appear in the glossary.

# Day to Night

When you look up at the sky, the sun always looks like it's in a different place. It takes an entire day to move across the sky. The sun comes up in the morning and goes away at night.

5

The sun may look like it moves, but it really stays in one place! It just looks like it moves because Earth rotates. When something rotates, it spins in a circle. Other things around it stay **fixed**.

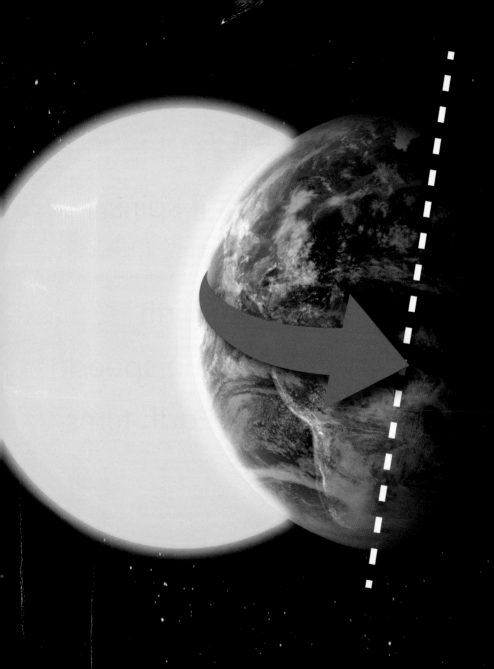

7

# The Changing Sky

We move with Earth as it spins, but we can't feel it. That's because everything on Earth moves with us at the same speed. The only way we know Earth turns is because the sky is always changing.

Earth spins around its **axis**. An axis is an imaginary line that passes through Earth from the North Pole to the South Pole. The spinning of Earth is called **rotation**. Earth's rotation is what gives us day and night.

11

# Sunrise

Earth rotates east. When we see the sun come up, it means we're rotating towards the sun. Not all places on Earth face east at the same time. This means day and night happen at different times around the world.

13

The sky changes as the sun begins to rise. As it rises, the sky goes from dark to light. First, we see part of the sun on the **horizon**. The sun gets higher and brighter as night turns into day.

15

# Sunset

At noon, the sun reaches its highest point in the sky. It looks big and bright. But, Earth keeps spinning! The sun gets lower in the sky as Earth rotates away from it. This is called a sunset.

17

Sunsets are very beautiful. They make pretty colors in the sky. The sunset looks red, yellow, and orange. Sometimes sunsets even look pink! Even after the sun goes down, we can still see the pretty colors.

19

# Moon and Stars

When the sun goes down, we can see the moon and stars. They give us light. They look like they move, too! Earth spins all night. In a few hours, the sun rises again!

# Sun Rising and Setting

**6:00**a.m.
The sun starts to rise.

**9:00**a.m.
The sun gets higher in the sky.

**12:00**p.m.
The sun reaches its highest point.

**3:00**p.m.
The sun gets lower in the sky.

**6:00**p.m.
The sun starts to set.

# Glossary

**axis:** an imaginary line through Earth from the North Pole to the South Pole

**fixed:** not moving

**horizon:** a line where Earth or the sea seems to meet the sky

**rotation:** one complete circle around a fixed point

# For More Information

## Books

Bailey, Jacqui. *Sun Up, Sun Down: The Story of Day and Night*. Minneapolis, MN: Picture Window Books, 2004.

Nelson, Robin. *Day and Night*. Minneapolis, MN: Lerner Publications Company, 2011.

## Websites

### The Rotation of the Earth

*www.kidsgeo.com/geography-for-kids/0018-the-rotation-of-the-earth.php*

Read about what happens when Earth moves.

### Why Does the Sun "Rise" and "Set"?

*www.learner.org/jnorth/tm/mclass/SunriseSetAns.html*

Read all about the sunrise and sunset.

# Index